SECRETS OF THE LOST ISLAND

Lynn Beach

Illustrations by Michael Racz

SCHOLASTIC INC.
New York Toronto London Auckland Sydney

To Kathleen and Harry Hartman

ISBN: 0-590-33233-3

 Published by Scholastic Inc. by arrangement with Parachute Press, Inc.

12 11 10 9 8 7 6 5 4 3 2 5 6 7 8 9/8

Printed in the U.S.A. 01

BEWARE!!!

DO NOT READ THIS BOOK FROM BEGINNING TO END!

You are about to embark on a strange voyage, a voyage that will lead you to a land of mystery—and danger. At the end of this voyage you may find yourself rich and famous, or you may be doomed to a watery grave. The choice is yours.

You will make your own decisions and choose your own paths by following the directions at the bottom of each page. What happens depends on you. If you get into trouble, turn back and choose a different path. If you're having a good time, keep going.

The secrets of Lost Island will work for you if you can stay sharp-witted in the face of frightening underwater creatures, a mad scientist's sinister plot, and all the untold perils of Lost Island. It is a challenge only the very bold should attempt.

Prepare for adventure as the secrets of Lost Island begin to unfold on PAGE 2.

Tall waves are crashing all around, drenching you with wet spray. You hear the first rumble of thunder from a storm.

The little cruiser *Louise* is tossing and jumping. You carefully make your way to the cabin, where your uncle Dave is trying desperately to turn the boat to shore.

"We'll never make it!" he shouts. "I'm going to head for that island."

Go on to the next page.

Only a few hours ago, the day was bright and calm. You were glad to help your uncle on this boating trip. You know it means a lot to him.

Several weeks ago, his wife, your aunt Louise, disappeared while swimming in these same waters. Now every weekend Dave takes his boat to look for Louise. He thinks she may be on one of the many deserted islands in the bay. Everyone else has given up hope—even the Coast Guard who searched for days. You think they are probably right. Still, you want to help Dave if there is even a slight chance she may be alive.

But now, both you and Dave are in serious trouble!

Water is everywhere. The boat is tilting at a crazy angle. You run back on deck. Up ahead are jagged rocks on the shore of the island. The waves are pushing you closer and closer.

What should you do? Should you hold on to the boat? Or will your chances be better if you try swimming for the island? Decide now—before the waves decide for you!

If you want to stay with the boat, go to PAGE 20.

If you think it is safer to swim for shore, go to PAGE 12.

You've got to get your flashlight. "Just a minute," you call out. Taking a deep breath, you bend down and start to crawl through the small opening. You stretch out your hands in front of you to feel for your flashlight.

You crawl further and further into the hole. There is no sign of your flashlight. You are about to turn back, but you stop. The ground beneath you is trembling slightly. The tremble grows and grows until the earth floor is rocking violently. Giant cracks begin to split the earth under you.

"Help!" you scream. "Help!"

"I'm coming," calls Dave. You hear him scrambling through the hole behind you. But the ground is crumbling rapidly and you start to fall. You realize that you are sliding, hands first, down a sheer rock face.

"Watch out!" you call to your uncle. Too late. The sharp crack of breaking rock pierces your ears. You realize Dave is falling too.

To see what awaits you at the bottom, turn to PAGE 26.

You decide to take your chances with the maze. Swimming strongly, you leave the lighted squid room, and the familiar current takes you into the darkness. Underwater channels open on each side of you as you try to follow the map in your head. You know that the grotto can be reached by taking the middle passage of the first turning.

It is easier to swim this time, and you know that you must be nearing the grotto. Now you come to a fork in the stream. You can't remember seeing this particular fork on the map. With growing horror, you realize that you are lost. But you must go on. You surface for a last deep breath, then make your choice.

If you decide to turn to the right, go to PAGE 46.

If you prefer to turn left, go to PAGE 31.

You are caught tightly in the folds of the net. Struggling only seems to make it pull tighter around you.

"Are you all right?" Dave asks.

"I think so," you say. "What do we do now?"

"There's a knife in my back pocket. If you can reach it, maybe we can cut our way out of here. If we fall, we'll land in the water."

You begin to hack at the net, but the material is strong and the pocket knife has little effect. Then you notice that the strands seem to be thinner near the top. You reach up and begin to cut them.

"Hurry up!" says Dave. "Someone is coming."

If you've never used a pocket knife in your life, turn to PAGE 53.

If you know how to handle a pocket knife, go to PAGE 44.

You decide to turn. But the sub is not responding. You can see the object ahead in the water. It is a large rock. It is getting closer and closer. Then, at the last second, the submarine turns to the right, missing it.

You and Dave breathe a sigh of relief. For hours you continue to glide through the sea. There is no radio to break the eerie silence. Whenever you are hungry, you eat peanut butter sandwiches. When you get tired, you take turns sleeping and operating the submarine.

You begin to lose track of time. If only you knew where you were! But the submarine goes on and on . . .

In boredom, you explore the submarine again. And then, to your surprise, you find something you had not noticed before. It is a small door in the wall in the back of the control room. You open it and let out a yell of excitement.

"Uncle Dave!" you cry. "Look at this!"

Behind the door is a large switch. Beneath it is a sign: PULL SWITCH TO SURFACE.

Pull the switch and turn to PAGE 13 to see what happens next.

The door opens with a hiss. When you step through, you are surprised by the sound of laughter. And then you stop and look around.

You are in a small, circular room. On the walls of the room are strange, round projections. Around the side of the room there are chairs. And seated in the chairs are strange creatures, each more bizarre than the other.

You see a mermaid, her flowing red hair decorated with seashells. Next to her is a blond, bearded pirate, picking his teeth with a knife. Across from the pirate is a man who looks like a nineteenth-century boat captain.

"What's going on here?" you say.

And at that moment a deep, booming voice cries, "Seize them!"

Two sailors, one with a peg leg, reach out and grab you and Dave, pinning your arms behind your backs.

"Well, well," says the deep voice. "What have we here?" Approaching you is a huge fat man, with an oily bald head.

"Who are you?" says Dave.

Go on to PAGE 88.

You pull the long switch. There is a brilliant flash of blue light. The lights in the room dim, then come back on. On the table, Aunt Louise sits up, looking puzzled. "What? Where am I?" she mutters.

"Louise, it's me, Dave," says Uncle Dave. Louise snaps out of her hazy state and suddenly recognizes you and Dave. A bright smile lights up her face and tears of joy begin to fill her eyes.

"I never thought I'd see either of you again," she cries, hugging the two of you. "I should have known you would save me!"

Suddenly Louise looks bewildered again. "I had the strangest dream," she says. "I was living under the ocean. I . . ."

"It's all right," Dave tells her. He helps her off the table. "I'll explain everything later. But for now, we've got to get out of here quickly."

You close your eyes and remember the map. "There are two ways out," you say. "One of them is straight ahead. According to the map, it goes to the beach. The other way is up those stairs to the boat basin."

Talk your choices over with Uncle Dave and Aunt Louise. Then prepare to make your escape.

If you decide to go back to the beach, turn to PAGE 38.

If you decide to try to get to the boat basin, go to PAGE 40.

"We won't do what you ask!" you say defiantly. Dr. Lamprey touches his belt again and raises the whip.

"How dare you defy me!" he shouts. His arm snakes back and the whip closes around your uncle's leg. To your horror, you watch as Dr. Lamprey flicks his arm again, and you see your uncle plunge into the boiling water.

"And now for you," mutters the evil doctor. Again his arm snakes back. In the next instant the whip catches you and flicks you into the pool.

You are boiling mad, but there is nothing more you can do now. Close the book quickly, to give yourself time to cool off.

THE END

You let go of the boat and fall into the water. You feel someone grab your arm, and realize that Dave has abandoned the boat, too.

The two of you swim for your lives, hoping you will reach the island. But the current has turned, and you see now that you are being swept away, toward the open ocean.

Suddenly, something bumps you from under the water. Your foot bangs against the cold, hard metal that is lifting you both out of the water. "What on earth?!" Dave mutters. You and Dave exchange looks of complete disbelief as you realize that a submarine is surfacing beneath you.

Terrified, you hold on. After a moment, the hatch opens. You look inside. You look back at the raging sea. There is really no choice. The two of you climb into the sub.

Turn to PAGE 62.

You pull the switch. To your delight it works. The submarine pops through the top of the water and sits floating on the waves, rocking from side to side. Excitedly, you and Dave go to the airlock and open the hatch.

All around you, as far as you can see, is brilliant blue water, capped with foamy waves. Through a cloudless sky shines a hot, tropical sun.

"I don't know where we are," says Dave. "But for sure this isn't the bay!"

Ahead, in the distance, is a tiny speck that might be an island. You go back to the control room. You don't know how to steer the submarine on the surface. But neither one of you wants to go underwater again, although it's the only way you feel confident running the submarine. How will you get to the island?

If you decide to go to the island underwater, turn to PAGE 76.

If you decide to try to steer the submarine above water, turn to PAGE 70.

You are more terrified than you have ever been in your life. But you can't leave Uncle Dave.

You hear a hissing noise. You turn to see that the pool is suddenly boiling. "Go ahead," Lamprey says. "Swim away. You'll be boiled like a lobster in thirty seconds. Now I'm losing patience. Will you get into my cage? Or must I use my whip?"

Will you enter the cage? Or will you try to fight the evil doctor?

If you go into the cage, turn to PAGE 59.

If you fight Dr. Lamprey, turn to PAGE 11.

You sit up with a start. You don't know what has awakened you—some noise, perhaps. It is just beginning to get light. You peer around the campsite and suddenly you realize that Uncle Dave is gone!

Alarmed, you stand up and look around. You can see his footprints faintly in the sand.

"Uncle Dave!" you call. There is no answer.

Your heart pounding, you follow his footprints along the beach. At last you see him in the distance, standing under a clump of trees. You run toward the trees.

"What's wrong?" you ask.

"Maybe nothing," says Dave. "When I woke up there was a man standing over me. He started running. I followed him . . . here."

Under the trees is a pool of greenish water. You can see fish swimming in it. But there is no sign of anyone or anything else.

"Where did he go?" you ask.

"I don't know," says Dave. "Maybe we ought to . . ."

But at that moment, a large fishing net drops over both of you. The next thing you know, you are pulled up into the trees, trapped.

Quick! Turn to PAGE 6.

You press the red button. For a moment nothing happens. Then you hear a deep rumbling noise.

Dr. Lamprey lets go of Louise. "Ignorant fool!" he shouts. "You've blown up the island!"

You hear the sound of an explosion and rocks begin falling all around you. Dave grabs your arm and you start to run, but water is pouring in from everywhere.

You, Dave, and Louise begin to swim as quickly as you can, away from the explosion. After a few minutes you find yourself in the open sea. In the distance, what is left of the island goes up in smoke and flames.

"We escaped from Dr. Lamprey," says Dave, gasping. "But we'll never make it to shore. It's too far."

Still, the three of you keep swimming. You are beginning to get very tired and cold when Louise suddenly says, "Look!"

You look up to see a sleek gray form in the water ahead of you. It is a very large dolphin. It begins talking in dolphin squeaks. There is something familiar about it.

Go on to PAGE 17.

The dolphin swims closer and squeaks at Aunt Louise.

Louise puts her arms around the dolphin. "It can help us swim to shore," she says.

"Don't trust it!" warns Uncle Dave. "It might be one of Dr. Lamprey's creatures!"

"Come on," says Louise. "Don't be afraid."

You and Uncle Dave exchange glances. Aunt Louise doesn't know how completely evil Dr. Lamprey was. But you are both tired and cold.

Should you let the dolphin help you? Or should you continue to swim, hoping that you will make it to shore on your own?

Turn to PAGE 35 if you decide to swim.

If you think you can trust the dolphin, go to PAGE 83.

The next morning, you and Dave get up early and begin to explore the island. You walk toward the small mountain at its center. At the top of the mountain, you see an opening to a cave. You decide to go inside.

It is cold and dark in the cave. Your flashlights make the gloom only a little brighter. Somewhere far off you hear water dripping. At one end of the narrow cave you spot a large passage that seems to lead to another room. At the back of the cave is an opening, barely big enough to crawl through. Now you notice something on the rocks just ahead of you.

"Come here," you call to Uncle Dave. "There is something written on the walls."

The two of you look at the strange writing. "I've never seen anything like this," Dave says. "I don't know what it means. But I can guess what *that* means." He points at a symbol above the writing.

Go on to PAGE 90.

RACZ

You decide to stay with the boat—but a wave suddenly lifts you and throws you onto the beach. You land with a THUD on cool, wet sand. In another minute Dave, still in the boat, comes crashing onto the rocks near the island. He jumps out of the boat and stumbles toward you. Both of you are shaken up, but not hurt.

The storm is over now, and you can see what is left of the boat washing ashore.

"We'd better make camp," Dave tells you. "Luckily, most of the supplies are in waterproof containers. But the radio is broken. I'll try to fix it in the morning."

Later, sitting around a cozy fire, your clothing dried out, you both feel better.

"This bay is known for danger," Uncle Dave tells you. "Sudden storms are common. For the past hundred years, many boats have disappeared around here. We were lucky."

He looks sad, and you know he is remembering Aunt Louise, who was not so lucky.

You decide to change the subject. "Where do you think we are?" you ask.

Dave hesitates. "I think we may be on Lost Island," he says with a worried look on his face.

Go on to PAGE 21.

In spite of the warmth of the fire, you feel a chill. "Wasn't there a big explosion on that island several years ago?" you ask.

"Yes," says Dave. "And there were rumors of all sorts of weird things going on there. The island was owned by a Dr. Lamprey. He was a very rich, very mysterious scientist. It was reported that he performed inhuman experiments. Animals were said to cringe or run away at the sight of him. After the explosion, he was never seen or heard from again."

"Do you think any of the stories were true?" you ask.

"Well, it's true that there was a gigantic explosion on the island. Louise and I saw the glow from the blast all the way from the mainland," says Dave. "And there was a Dr. Lamprey who lived there. But I don't think we'll meet any ghosts or talking sea creatures." He smiles reassuringly, but his face is still concerned. You fall asleep and dream of mermaids.

What happens when you wake up? That all depends on how soundly you sleep!

If you are an insomniac who finds it very difficult to sleep through the night, turn to PAGE 49.

If you are a sound sleeper, then turn to PAGE 18.

If you are a light sleeper who wakes at every sound, then turn to PAGE 15.

"Quick!" says the tortoise. "Climb on my back and hold tight. Get ready for some splashing."

You help Dave to climb onto the tortoise's back. Then you climb on yourself. The shell is slippery, and it takes you several tries. At last you succeed by grabbing hold of the torch on the turtle's back. You and Dave both hold on to the torch for dear life as the tortoise slides into the water and begins to paddle.

"You are lucky it was I who found you," he says. "Most visitors are greeted by the slaves of Dr. Lamprey. And they never leave here alive."

"But where . . ." you start to ask.

"Be quiet," says the tortoise. "I must concentrate on my swimming. I know where you will be safe. And I will take you there. But you must be quiet. And you must trust me. Now hold your breath and prepare to get wet!"

With that, the tortoise dives under the water. The torch goes out with a hiss. Water closes around your face, and you hold on for dear life as the tortoise begins to swim underwater. Just as you think you can hold your breath no longer, the tortoise breaks into the air.

Turn to PAGE 91.

You step into a long, low room with metal walls and floor. The room is furnished with a metal table and chairs, but that is all. Your footsteps echo metallically whenever you take a step.

"Hello?" calls Dave. "Is anyone here?"

The only answer is an echo: ". . . here . . . here . . . here . . ."

You and Dave continue to explore the sub. You find a room containing bunks for sleeping. You find a galley. It is stocked with peanut butter and bread. But you don't find any other people.

The last room you explore is the control room. Through a tiny, thick window you can see the green sea outside.

You and Dave look at each other. "I guess it's time to learn how to drive this thing," he says.

The only problem is that neither of you has any idea how to run a submarine.

The two of you study the complicated control panel. There are dials and gauges, switches and lights. Two large red buttons on the panel are labeled MANUAL and AUTOMATIC.

Go on to PAGE 25.

Dave shrugs. "Your guess is as good as mine," he says. "Which one shall we try?"

Think it over carefully. If you decide to put the submarine on automatic control, press the AUTOMATIC *button and turn to page 60.*

If you want to put the sub on manual power, press the MANUAL *button and turn to PAGE 51.*

You fall face-down on a sandy beach. Near your head you can hear the sound of the tide washing in and out. You pick yourself up and realize that there are no bones broken.

"Uncle Dave?" you call. "Are you all right?"

You hear a groan next to you. In the dim light you see that Uncle Dave has a cut over his eyebrow, and he seems to be dazed.

Looking around, you discover that you are in an underwater cave. Thick moss grows on the walls above you. Water drips everywhere. Suddenly, your eyes are dazzled by torchlight. Standing over you is the biggest sea tortoise you have ever seen. Strapped to its back is a glowing torch.

"Who dares to invade the underwater kingdom of Dr. Lamprey?" asks the tortoise.

You stare at the sea creature in shock. How can a tortoise speak? You think of hidden microphones, but the voice seems to belong to the creature itself. Before you can think what to do next, the tortoise speaks again.

"You are in worse trouble than you can imagine," it says. "But you can trust me. Climb onto my back, and I will try to help you escape."

Go on to PAGE 27.

What do you do? You know you can easily outrun the tortoise. But Uncle Dave is still dazed and you are worried about him. Should you trust the tortoise and let him help you and Uncle Dave?

If you decide to trust the tortoise, turn to PAGE 22.

If you decide to try to make a run for it instead, go to PAGE 45.

"I'm sorry I scared you," says the squid. "I thought you wanted to play. Are you all right? I've been alone in here so long I've forgotten my manners."

You can't believe your ears — a talking squid! "How did you learn to talk?" you ask. "Only humans can talk."

"I used to be just as human as you," says the squid. "In fact, all the creatures here were — till Dr. Lamprey got hold of us."

"What did he do to you?" you ask.

"He's an evil genius," says the squid. "A very long time ago, he built a machine. Somehow, it can take a human being's personality and switch it with the personality of a sea creature."

"But that's impossible!" you say. Or is it?

Go on to PAGE 29 and find out.

"I thought so, too," says the squid. "Till it happened to me. I used to be a fisherman. One day I was shipwrecked on the island. Dr. Lamprey found me and put me in his machine. The next thing I knew I was here."

"That's terrible!" you say, shocked.

"What's worse is that he keeps the bodies of changed humans in glass cages," says the squid.

You suddenly remember the woman who looked like your Aunt Louise. "Can you be changed back to a human?" you ask.

"Dr. Lamprey controls us with a special belt," says the squid. "But he doesn't bother to change anyone back. When he tires of us he freezes our molecules. That turns us into living statues."

You realize that you must get back to the grotto and try to rescue Dave before he is turned into a sea creature — or worse. You tell the squid your problem.

"I think I can help you," it says. "Behind you on the cave wall is a map of Dr. Lamprey's underwater lab. I drew it when I first came here."

You turn to look at the wall. Scratched into it is a crudely-drawn map. Turn to PAGE 30 and study the map. You must try to memorize it.

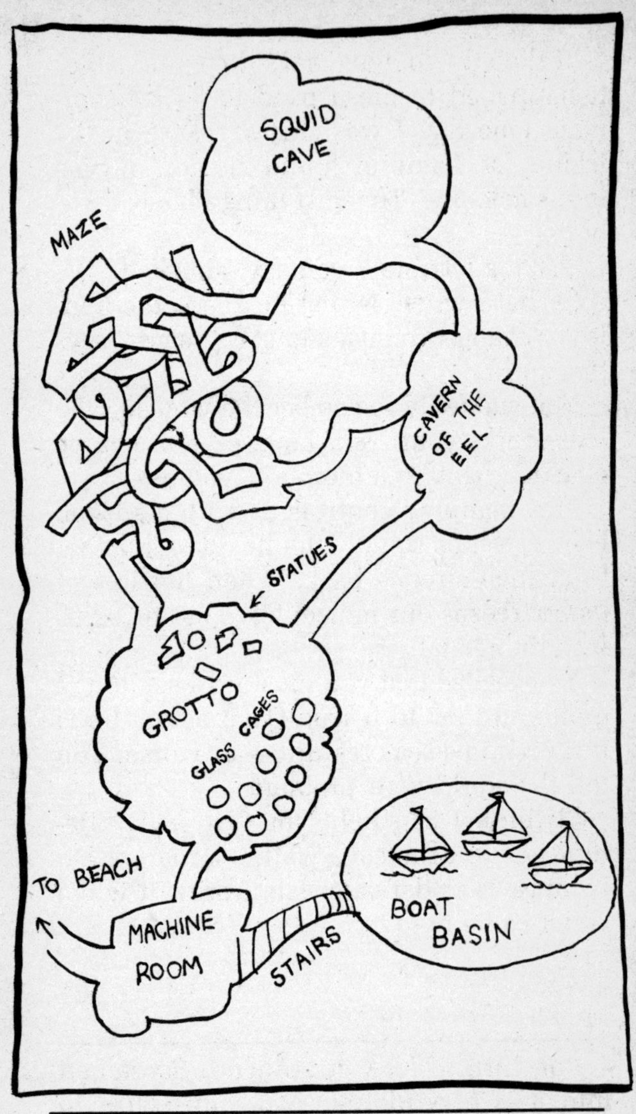

After you study the map, turn to PAGE 54.

You turn to the left, and through the murky water you can see a shining, shimmery door ahead. There are ivory pillars on either side. You think that this must be the door to the grotto.

Relieved, you swim through the opening. Your feet touch bottom and you stand, prepared to walk out of the water. But then you notice that the ground beneath you is soft — very soft. In fact, it doesn't feel like ground at all. It feels like a tongue.

And now you turn around and notice that the door is closing behind you. Too late, you realize that it wasn't a door at all, but the mouth of a giant fish. And the ivory pillars were large, sharp teeth.

Too bad! But cheer up. After all, the story of Jonah was always one of your favorites.

THE END

"This is the end of the ride," says the tortoise. It leans to one side and you and Dave slide off its back. "Just step through the door. You will be safe enough here."

You hesitate. Uncle Dave is now standing beside you, but you can see he is still weak.

At that moment the tortoise speaks again. Its beady eyes gleam red in the eerie flickering light. "I would advise you to do as I say," it insists. "You cannot get out of here without help."

"We're not getting into a cage!" you say.

You look around the grotto. Behind the cages are stone statues of fish and exotic sea creatures. You cannot see any way out except through the pool where you came in.

"Come on," says Dave, his voice still weak. "Let's make a swim for it!"

At that moment you see something that freezes your blood. In one of the cages, sitting quietly, is a woman who looks exactly like Aunt Louise!

Go on to PAGE 33.

"Uncle Dave," you start to say. But before you can finish you hear a large CRACK!

You turn to see a huge, powerful man with a head as bald as an egg. He is holding a whip in his hand.

"Not so fast!" says the giant bald man. "No one escapes from Dr. Lamprey!"

He cracks his whip again and Uncle Dave falls to the wet, slippery rock floor.

"Go on!" calls Dave. "Get out of here! I'll be all right!"

You look again at the big man with the whip, and at your uncle, lying helpless on the floor. Now you must decide what to do. Should you try to get away and maybe find help? Or should you stay and help Uncle Dave? Decide quickly.

If you decide to stay with your uncle, turn to PAGE 14.

If you decide to get away, take a deep breath, dive into the water, and turn to PAGE 92.

"Forget it, Lamprey," you say. "You can't make us do anything." You're not cooperating with this kook.

"You'll regret this!" Dr. Lamprey says. "Put them in irons!"

You struggle, but soon the sailors have handcuffed you and Dave to an iron railing in a small, dark, windowless cabin.

You can feel the submarine diving. Its engines sound loud as it roars along. At last it begins to surface again.

Neither you nor Dave says anything, but you know you are both very, very scared. What will happen to you now?

You find out soon enough. The two sailors open the door, and without a word take off your handcuffs. Then they force you through the submarine and up the ladder to the hatch.

They push you out of the hatch. It is darkest night, and you can hear water splashing as you fall from the top of the submarine.

To find out what awaits you at the bottom, turn to PAGE 65.

"Come on," says Dave. "Let's swim for it!"

He pulls Aunt Louise away from the dolphin. But the dolphin doesn't want to let her go.

In fact, it doesn't want to let any of you go. And it is much stronger than you. Using its snout, it pushes and carries you along. Soon you give up arguing — you need all your breath for swimming.

The sky is growing light again when you find yourselves washing up on a sandy beach. At first the three of you just lie there in the surf, exhausted.

When you have gotten your strength back, you see that the dolphin has gone. You also see that there is something strangely familiar about this island. Although you can hear birds singing, the island seems to be completely deserted. In its center is a small mountain shaped like a cone.

But Lost Island was destroyed in the explosion — or was it? And as for Dr. Lamprey . . .

You help Dave and Louise gather firewood to make a signal fire. And you try not to think about the fact that you seem to be back where you started out a dozen adventures ago!

THE END

You follow Dave into the next room. "I lost my flashlight," you say.

"Luckily there's another one at camp," says Dave. "But look at this."

You look where he is pointing and you forget all about your flashlight. This room is much larger than the other one. Along the back wall there are dozens of stone sculptures of sea creatures. There are giant fish of every sort, their stone fins curving eerily in the air. There is a shark, and a huge ray, and many fish you do not recognize. There is even a mermaid, with long, curly stone hair.

"Who do you suppose made these?" you ask in a whisper.

"There's no way to know," says Dave. "But Dr. Lamprey was said to be an artist. These are beautiful. I'm going to photograph them."

He hands you his flashlight while he gets his camera ready. Suddenly there is an ominous rumbling sound. Bits of stone start to fall to the floor of the cave.

"It's a cave-in!" Dave shouts. "Quick! Go back the way we came!"

Go on to PAGE 37.

Your uncle is choking from the dust and can't see as well as you can. He starts to move back to the opening. But you can see that the rocks are falling faster there. You think it may be safer by the statues.

Quick! Make a decision. If you think it is safer to try to get out of the cave, follow Uncle Dave and turn to PAGE 43.

If you think it is safer to stand by the statues, grab your uncle's arm and pull him with you. Then turn to PAGE 50.

You decide to head for the beach. The three of you enter the dark passage straight ahead. It is steep and seems to be leading upward. At the top, you think you can see daylight. You have almost reached the top when a shadow falls across the entrance.

You are shocked to see Dr. Lamprey standing there.

But you are not as shocked as Dr. Lamprey himself. "How did you escape?" he cries.

You are close enough to touch him. And you realize that this is your chance to get rid of the evil scientist once and for all.

But what is the best way to stop him? You still have the Mediterranean Magnet and the poison ink. Which should you use? Make your choice quickly, before he uses his belt.

If you decide to use the Mediterranean Magnet, turn to PAGE 69.

If you choose to use the poison ink, turn to PAGE 78.

"Well?" asks Dave. "What are they worth?"

The professor begins to chuckle. "I suppose they might be worth a few dollars—to a museum."

"What do you mean?" you cry. "These coins are gold!"

"They're brass," says the professor. "And they're not even real coins. But I must say they are some of the most remarkable examples I have ever seen—of ancient counterfeit coins!"

"Counterfeit?" you echo. With a sinking feeling you realize that you're not going to be rich after all. But maybe a museum will buy the coins. And then maybe Uncle Dave can get another boat. And then maybe, just maybe, you'll get to go on another adventure . . . and another . . . and another.

THE END (FOR NOW)

You figure that the boat basin is your safest bet. Leading upward toward the basin are ancient-looking stone steps, covered with seaweed and slime. The three of you begin the slippery climb as quietly as you can.

Soon you hear the sound of the surf, and suddenly you break into the open air. Ahead of you is the boat basin. There are boats and ships of all kinds there: a yacht, a rowboat, a submarine, even a canoe. There is also a cabin cruiser that looks very much like the *Louise*.

"The keys are in the cruiser," says Dave. "But it might make too much noise. Maybe we ought to take the rowboat instead."

The three of you talk it over. Which boat will you use to make your escape from Lost Island?

If it's the rowboat, turn to PAGE 82.
If it's the cruiser, turn to PAGE 56.

Holding your breath, you begin to swim into the lighted passage. You lift your head above water and see that there are steep banks on both sides. Above you is a rocky ceiling, glowing with bright fluorescent colors.

Suddenly, something grabs your leg and tries to drag you under. Frantically, you try to pull free, but the grip only tightens. The thing that has hold of you begins to tug you to the bottom. You are running out of air. Again you try to break free. You struggle, but it grips your other leg, and then your arms.

Just when you think you've met your end, there is a sudden WHOOSH! and you feel yourself being thrown onto wet sand. For a moment all you can do is gasp for air. Then you look around and realize that you are on a small beach beneath the stone cliffs of an underwater cave.

You look for the creature that grabbed you and suddenly find yourself gazing into the clear amber eye of a giant squid!

To find out what happens next, turn to PAGE 28.

You look sadly at the necklace. But your air supply is just too low. Holding the bag of gold coins, you head back to the submarine.

Three days later, you and Uncle Dave are standing in the office of a professor at the university. You don't even want to think about all the trouble you had getting the submarine home. There were too many close calls. And you especially don't want to remember trying to explain how you got the submarine in the first place.

For now, all you can think about is the gold coins. You are sure that they are going to make you and Dave very, very rich.

The professor is studying the coins carefully with a magnifying glass.

"Remarkable!" he says. "Remarkable, remarkable!"

Each time he says "remarkable," you imagine another million dollars in your bank account.

At last he has finished examining them. He sets the bag of coins on his desk.

Go to PAGE 39.

You and Dave run for the entrance of the cave. The rubble from the falling rocks makes it impossible to see. The ominous rumbling is growing louder and louder.

You make it through the opening into the first room of the cave. You almost make it to the cave entrance. But the cave-in has now become too big to stop, and you realize that the whole mountain is about to fall in on you and your uncle.

The last thing you hear, before you hear no more, is an evil chuckling . . . and you realize that the stories about Dr. Lamprey were, perhaps, true after all.

THE END

You hear the heavy footsteps of someone approaching. Even more quickly, you cut at the strands. One parts, then two, then three, and suddenly you are free—but not for long.

You land in the water, as you had expected, which is okay, because both you and Dave are good swimmers. Unfortunately, what you didn't expect is that the fish you saw in the pond were piranhas.

And they are very hungry.

Close the book now, before the main course begins.

THE END

"Come on, Dave!" you shout. "Let's make a run for it!"

"Trust me!" calls the tortoise.

"Not in a million years!" you shout. You look behind to see the animal clumsily following. Then there is a splashing sound and you see the tortoise disappearing into the water . . . which you suddenly realize is rising.

The small amount of sand quickly disappears as the water covers it. You begin to tread water, helping Uncle Dave stay afloat. But it is obvious that the entire cave will soon be filled with water. Before it closes over your head completely, you yell out, "Oh, tortoise, I believe you now. I was only fooling!" But it is too late. This is . . .

THE END

You decide to turn right. Soon your head breaks through the water, and you realize that you are nearing a narrow beach. Ahead of you is a small opening. Beyond the opening is a faint glow and the sound of electricity crackling. You realize that you have come to the Cavern of the Eel.

To find out what awaits you there, climb out of the water and turn to PAGE 67.

Dr. Lamprey is gone for the moment, but you know that from now on you are in terrible danger. Quickly, you tell Dave where you have been and everything you have learned. You explain what has happened to Aunt Louise.

"I knew she was still alive," he says sadly. "But now her mind is in the body of a sea creature."

"If we can find Dr. Lamprey's machine, we may be able to bring her back," you say.

You open the door to Aunt Louise's cage. The woman inside makes strange squeaking noises. She sounds just like a dolphin.

"We're here to help you, Louise," says Dave. He picks her up. She slithers in his arms, then relaxes. She seems to trust him.

Now you think back to the map. Through the door ahead should be the machine room. Stealthily, you and Dave enter it.

Go on to PAGE 48.

The room is filled with scientific equipment. In the center of the room is a large machine. Long electrodes lead from it to a metal cap. A control panel stands above it. Set in the control panel is a glowing blue gem that looks like the Mediterranean Magnet. Next to the gem are two switches. One is long and one is short.

Uncle Dave sets Aunt Louise down on the table. She smiles and makes more squeaking noises. You sense that she remembers the machine.

Now, quickly, you and Dave place the cap with the electrodes over her head.

Nervously, you approach the panel. You touch the magnet to the blue gem. The machine hums to life, the lights on its panel blinking. Then you pull one of the switches.

If it's the short switch, turn to PAGE 80.
If it's the long switch, turn to PAGE 10.

You are awakened by a chilly breeze blowing from the sea. The sky is inky dark. Hundreds of glittering stars provide a shimmering light.

You sit up and pull your blanket tighter around you, remembering how you got here. In the distance you hear the wail of a fire engine. You start to lie down again, and then sit bolt upright.

A fire engine? On a deserted island?

Quickly you scramble to your feet and follow the sound. Soon you can see flames shooting up into the sky. A crowd has gathered as a giant skyscraper burns.

You approach and watch, fascinated. The water from the fire hoses splashes over the crowd. You feel yourself getting soaked.

And then you realize that you really are soaked. The fire engines and fire were only a dream. But the water, which is now over your head, isn't.

Before you go under for the third time, you realize sadly that you have learned a valuable lesson. Never go sleepwalking on a beach at night.

THE END

You and Uncle Dave huddle beneath the stone statues as the roof of the cave begins to fall in. Through the noise of falling rubble you hear an evil chuckling. Maybe it is only your imagination. You hope so.

The stones are falling thicker and faster. You hear a loud CRACK! and watch as the mermaid's tail breaks off and bounces off the stone walls.

Through the thick stone dust you see a crack appear in the floor of the cave. "Uncle Dave," you call, "watch out!"

But before you can finish your warning, the floor of the cave collapses. You lose sight of your uncle, and you feel yourself falling through the air.

Turn to PAGE 26.

You press the MANUAL button and the motor whirrs to life. The lights on the control panel start blinking. The submarine is moving!

You and Uncle Dave begin to experiment with the controls. You figure out how to make the submarine go forward and backward. You figure out how to make the sub turn. But you cannot figure out how to make it go up.

Suddenly a large red light on the control panel begins flashing on and off. A siren goes off and a sign lights up: OBJECT STRAIGHT AHEAD!

What do you do now? Make a decision quickly!

If you decide to turn left or right, go to PAGE 7.

If you think it is safer to go down, press the DIVE *button and turn to PAGE 60.*

If you decide to reverse course, turn to PAGE 74.

Frantically, you begin to saw at the top strands of the net. But nervousness has made your hands sweaty. The knife drops from your grasp, landing in the water below with a forlorn PLOP!

You hear a deep, booming laugh. Through the spaces in the net you see a tall man with a thick black beard approaching through the sand. He is dressed in gaudy bright colors. Gold rings glisten in his ear, and a sharp-looking sword is attached to a red sash at his waist.

"Yo, ho, ho," he says. "Looks like I caught me a couple of fish!"

"Let us go!" says Dave.

The man only laughs harder.

"We'll have to be very careful," Dave whispers to you. "This man is obviously insane. He's seems to think he's a pirate."

"I got good ears, too," the man says, grinning wickedly. "And I ain't insane. In fact, I'm Hedwick the Pirate, terror of the Seven Seas."

"There haven't been any pirates in this area for a hundred years," says Dave.

Go to PAGE 89.

"I have memorized the map," you tell the squid. "I know I don't have much of a chance, but I'm going to try."

"There are only two ways to overcome Dr. Lamprey," says the squid. "One is to get his belt. Without it, he is powerless."

"How can that be done?" you ask.

"The best way is to get the Mediterranean Magnet from the electric eel that guards it," says the squid. "But the only way to get the magnet is to guess the eel's secret. Many people have perished trying to get the magnet."

"What's the other way?" you ask.

Turn to PAGE 93 and find out.

You approach Dave's cage, moving as quickly and quietly as you can. At first you can see no way to open it, but then you notice that the catch is sealed with a blue stone that looks very much like the Mediterranean Magnet.

Could it be? you wonder. Cautiously you reach out with the ring and touch the magnet to the stone.

Instantly, the glass door springs open and Dave steps out.

The two of you immediately turn to confront Dr. Lamprey.

But he is not there. While you were opening the door, he somehow escaped. And if he was watching, he now knows that you have the magnet.

Turn to PAGE 47.

The cruiser's engine jumps to life and soon Lost Island is just a speck in the distance.

"I can't believe we escaped so easily," says Aunt Louise.

"What makes you think you did?" says a deep, booming voice that seems to come from thin air. At that moment the cruiser begins to shake and the motor starts sputtering. The boat stops dead in the water.

A cabinet opens and out steps Dr. Lamprey. You reach for the Mediterranean Magnet, but you find you can't move. Dr. Lamprey is pressing one of the buttons on his belt.

"You've given me more trouble than I expected," he says to the three of you. "But you're in my power now. I'm not going to waste any more time with you. You'll all become sea creatures — starting with you!"

He points at you. Then he presses another button on his belt.

Go on to PAGE 57.

The power of Dr. Lamprey's belt throws you overboard. The water closes over your face. You begin to move your fins. You look up at the cruiser and see that Dave is struggling with Dr. Lamprey. You are only mildly interested in the outcome of the fight, because you are suddenly very, very hungry. Hungrier than you have ever been. You are as hungry as a shark. In fact — you are a shark!

There is a sudden SPLASH! and you are now more interested. It seems that Dr. Lamprey has fallen overboard. How handy, you think. And just in time for dinner.

You swim over to where the evil scientist is struggling, trying to climb back in the boat. You don't realize until after you have eaten Dr. Lamprey that you also ate the belt. And it was your only chance to turn back into a human.

For a few minutes you feel sad. You will miss Uncle Dave and Aunt Louise. But soon your mind turns to more important matters . . . like where you're going to find your next meal.

THE END

58

You guess that the eel is wearing less than 100 rings. You shout out your answer.

"Too bad," says the eel. "I have many more rings than that. And each one of them was formed from the remains of someone who made an unlucky guess."

You begin to edge toward the door.

"Now hold still. This won't hurt at all." The eel begins to glow more brightly as it prepares to hurl a bolt of electricity at you. Sadly, you realize that this story has now come to a shocking . . .

THE END

You help Dave to stand up. He has to lean on you for support as you walk toward the glass cage. The evil doctor is chuckling behind you.

Just as you pass Dr. Lamprey, Dave stumbles and starts to fall forward. You see him wink, and you know he has a plan.

He falls heavily against Dr. Lamprey. As he does, you see his hand press the button on the evil scientist's belt. There is a whooshing noise, and the water stops boiling.

The two men fall to the floor. Dave grabs the whip as he wrestles with Dr. Lamprey. Cool water is pouring into the pool from the outside passage.

"Go now!" Dave calls to you. "Swim for your life! It's the only chance we have!"

You don't want to leave him, but you see there is no choice. You take a deep breath and dive into the now-cool water.

Go to PAGE 92.

You press the button. The engine roars and the submarine suddenly begins to sink down . . . down . . . down and then THUMP. It lands on the bottom of the sea. You and Dave look out the round window and ahead you can see the remains of a sunken sailing ship! Its rotting masts sway gently in the underwater current. Fish of every color and shape swim in and out through the holes in its side.

Beside one of the holes lies a rotting iron box. Spilling from its half-open top are what appear to be gold coins!

"Look, Dave!" you say. "Sunken treasure!"

"Too bad we can't go get it," he says.

"But we can!" you say. "There's a diving suit in one of the lockers. And I bet that gold is worth a fortune."

"That suit is too small for me," says Dave. "And I don't think it's safe for you to go out there."

But you are determined. Eventually, you talk Dave into letting you go after the treasure. You carefully put on the suit. The air-supply gauge reads half full. Now, close the airlock, and open the hatch.

Then turn to PAGE 75 to see what happens next.

RACZ 84

Darkness surrounds you inside the submarine. You and Dave look around. On two of the shiny metal walls are doors, secured with large round handles.

You can hear a ghostly clanging coming from far off.

You look longingly at the sky beyond the open hatch. "Maybe we ought to . . ." you start to say. But at that moment the hatch begins to close, locking you in.

You and Dave talk it over. You don't know what is awaiting you behind the closed doors. But you know you will go crazy sitting here in the dark, listening to ghostly clanging sounds. The only remaining question is, which door do you open?

If you choose to open the round door, turn to PAGE 24.

If you prefer the rectangular door, turn to PAGE 8.

At the end of the rock slide you stand up and shake yourself dry. You look around and realize that you are back in the grotto. The same glass cages are there, and the same weird stone statues.

In the nearest cage is a familiar face. It is Aunt Louise! She has a blank stare on her face. Her mind must be somewhere in the body of a sea creature.

Then you see something that fills you with horror. In the next cage is Uncle Dave! When he sees you, his lips move, but you cannot hear him through the glass.

You breathe a sigh of relief. He hasn't been turned into a sea creature—yet!

Uncle Dave now raps gently on the glass and points. You turn and look to see that Dr. Lamprey is stretched out on a cot behind you, fast asleep.

This is your perfect chance to get rid of Dr. Lamprey. But he is much bigger than you. Maybe it would be safer to let Dave out of the cage first.

Quick! Make a decision.

If you decide to attack Dr. Lamprey, turn to PAGE 68.

If you decide to free Dave first, turn to PAGE 55.

You decide that there is just enough time to get the necklace before your air runs out. Quickly, you kneel down and begin to pull it from the mud. But it seems to be stuck on something. You lean closer, and then you feel a tug. Somehow your air hose has become tangled up with the skeleton.

Your air gauge now reads EMPTY. You immediately forget all about the necklace. Frantically, you try to pull your air hose away from the skeleton. But you cannot untangle it. It's almost as if the skeleton were deliberately holding on.

As you take your last gasp of air, you realize that soon there will be two skeletons guarding the treasure.

THE END

As you tumble off the submarine into the water, a strong current pulls you down, down, down. This is surely the end of both of you. But wait! A tremendous suction pulls you from the ocean floor. You and Dave are swept into what seems to be a long metal tunnel. The suction shoots you up into a shallow pool. The water in the pool is warm. There is an odd, fishy smell in the air.

Suddenly, a harsh barking sound makes you both jump. It's so dark that you can't see where the noise is coming from. You can't even see each other.

All at once you are blinded by a bright light that is snapped on overhead. "What's going on here?" yells a man wearing a night watchman's uniform.

You look around you. On all sides are seals! Excited by the commotion, the seals are leaping around and swimming in circles. Then you realize what has happened. You and Dave got caught up in the pipe that leads to the city aquarium! You are in the seal room!

This all starts to seem very funny to you and Dave. You begin flipping around and making seal noises. No—you're not crazy. You are just happy that your nightmare adventure has finally come to . . .

THE END

Holding your breath, you plunge once again into the dark current. The water is suddenly flowing more swiftly. You rise to the surface to get some air. To your horror, you realize that there are no air pockets in this passage! You can't breathe!

You hold your breath as long as you can, and then you hold it a second longer. Your last thought as you lapse into unconsciousness is to wonder where the current will come out.

Will you be luckier next time? The only way to tell is to open the book and dive into another adventure!

THE END

You step through the opening into the Cavern of the Eel. Suspended from the ceiling, stalactites glow in every color of the rainbow. In the center of the room a huge snakelike creature is coiled. Its body is covered with dozens of gold rings, each set with precious jewels. Surrounding it is a halo of blue light, and you realize that it must be the electric eel.

The eel begins to uncoil, then speaks in a crackling voice. "Halt!" it says. "State your business."

"I am looking for the Mediterranean Magnet," you say, trying to keep your voice from shaking.

"Many travelers before you have tried to get this magnet," laughs the eel. "But no one has ever guessed my secret. If you can guess correctly, I will give it to you." The eel pauses, then continues: "How many rings do I have on my body?"

You study the eel, frowning. There seem to be about ten rings for each foot of the eel's length. The part of the eel you can see is at least six feet long. But the rest of his body is coiled away. Make a guess now. Make the best estimate you can.

If you guess 100 or fewer rings, turn to PAGE 58.

If you guess more than 100 rings, turn to PAGE 72.

You think it best to get Lamprey while you have the chance. Stealthily you approach the sleeping scientist. Most people look innocent when they sleep, but Dr. Lamprey looks evil, his bald head glistening in the eerie light of the grotto.

Your best chance is to get his belt. You take the ring off your arm and bring it closer to him. Just as you are about to touch the buckle, Dr. Lamprey's eyes snap open.

He is quick for such a big man, and he rolls out of the way. Now he stands menacingly, his hand poised over the belt.

"Welcome back to my grotto!" he laughs. "You left in such a hurry that I didn't have time to welcome you properly. But now you will be my guest—forever!"

What should you do now!? You still have the poison ink—but what's the best way to use it? It's your last and only hope!

If you want to stall Dr. Lamprey until you figure out a way to use the ink, turn to PAGE 79.

If you decide to use the ink right now, turn to PAGE 77.

You decide to use the Mediterranean Magnet. Before Dr. Lamprey can move, you pull off the ring and touch the blue gem to the buckle on his belt. With a loud click the belt opens and falls to the sand. He tries to grab it, but you are quicker. You fasten it around your waist.

Dr. Lamprey has grown pale. "Give that back!" he cries. "It's dangerous! You don't know what you are doing!"

"Come on," you say to your aunt and uncle. "We're getting out of here."

Suddenly Dr. Lamprey grabs Aunt Louise. He holds a knife to her throat.

"Give me back the belt," he says. "Or your aunt will die!"

"Don't trust him!" yells Dave. "Use the belt!"

You agree that the belt is your best chance. But you don't know how it works. Beside the buckle there are three colored buttons. In desperation, you decide to press one of them.

If you press the orange button, turn to PAGE 73.

If you press the red button, turn to PAGE 16.

If you press the green button, turn to PAGE 81.

It's easier than you expected to steer on the surface. As the submarine approaches the island, you see that it is covered with palm trees. You cannot see any buildings. Suddenly, the engine begins to cough and sputter. Then the submarine stops.

"We seem to have run out of fuel," says Dave. "Let's hope the people on this island are friendly."

You dive into the waves and swim the short distance to the island. The beach is white and spotless. There is a single set of footprints leading from the beach to the nearest grove of trees.

"There's someone here," says Dave.

At that moment a figure steps out from behind a coconut palm. You cannot believe your eyes. It is your aunt Louise!

She runs up to you, and she and Dave hug each other. Both are full of questions.

"How did you get here?" Dave asks.

Go to PAGE 87.

There have to be more than 100 rings there, you estimate. You tell the eel your guess. Its coils begin to shake, and the rings clank together with a sound like bells.

At first you are afraid that you have failed, but then you realize that the eel is laughing.

"Well done," it says when it gets its breath. "No one has ever out-guessed me before. Well, I was getting tired of guarding the magnet." With a quick movement it flips a ring off its tail. Set into the ring is a glowing blue gem.

You pick up the ring, puzzled.

"The magnet's power is centered in the gem," says the eel. "Now slip the ring on your arm and guard it well."

"How does it work?" you ask.

"When the time comes, you must get close enough to Dr. Lamprey to touch the buckle on his belt with the magnet. When you do, the belt will automatically unlock."

"Thank you," you say. You review the map in your head, then walk to the back of the cavern. Below you is a long rock slide, leading through a waterfall. Holding your breath, you sit and begin the long slide down.

To see what awaits you at the bottom, turn to PAGE 63.

You press the orange button. For a moment nothing happens. Dr. Lamprey is still standing there, still holding a knife to Aunt Louise's throat.

What if the belt didn't work? You are about to try one of the other buttons when Dave says, "Look!"

As you watch, Dr. Lamprey begins to topple over. He has become stiff as a statue. Louise easily wiggles out of his grasp.

Now the evil scientist lies on the ground, his arm curved, his frozen fingers holding a knife.

"Another statue for his collection," says Dave with satisfaction. "And now, let's get out of here!"

Turn to PAGE 86.

You try to reverse course. The submarine begins to shake all over. Now more lights blink and another siren goes off. A flashing sign reads: OBJECT IN BACK!

Quickly, you and Dave try to turn the sub. You begin pressing switches—any switches!

But it is too late. With a shuddering crash, the submarine comes to a stop. Water begins to pour into the control room.

Alas, you have learned a valuable lesson too late: It's not safe to drive a submarine without a license.

THE END

You feel weightless as you walk from the submarine to the sunken ship. Ghostly shadows move all around you. There is a sudden movement in front of you. You jump back. But it is only a rose-colored fish.

As you approach the sunken chest, you see that it is guarded by an ancient human skeleton. The bones sway back and forth in the sea current. It seems almost alive.

You are beginning to think that maybe it wasn't such a good idea to come out here after all.

You scoop up the coins and put them into a bag that you brought along. Soon the bag is nearly full.

You look at your air gauge. You are shocked to see it is almost empty. Better hurry back to the sub.

A sudden gleam catches your eye. You see, half-buried in the mud, a beautiful necklace. It looks as if it is made of diamonds. Maybe you can get it before your air runs out. And maybe you can't.

What do you do? Do you take a few extra seconds to dig the necklace out of the mud? If so, turn to PAGE 64.

If you think it is safer to take your bag of coins back to the sub, turn to PAGE 42.

You play it safe and go back under the water. Now that you know how to resurface, you're not worried. Smoothly, the sub surfaces at the edge of the island. Up close, you can see that the island is fairly big. All along the shore you see anchored ships. The ships are flying the flag of the United States.

"We've found a Navy base!" says Dave, surprised.

You don't stop to wonder how you are going to explain your presence here, let alone where you got the submarine.

You only know that you can't wait to stand on dry land again!

THE END

Desperation makes you bold.

"Don't move!" you say in a commanding tone. Surprised, Dr. Lamprey stops and stares at you. Now you pull out the bottle of poisoned ink that the squid gave you. "If you touch the belt, I'll throw this at you!" You draw your arm back, ready to throw.

Dr. Lamprey's eyes widen in horror.

"Where did you get that?" he demands.

"Never mind," you say. You are very pleased at how well your plan is working. You are about to demand that Dr. Lamprey open Dave's cage when he suddenly touches one of the buttons on his belt. There is a puff of smoke, and he is gone.

You look around, but it is too late. "You've won this round," says Lamprey's fading voice. "But you'll never get out alive!"

You realize that you must move quickly now. You put the ink back in your pocket and hurry over to Dave's cage. You twist the handle and the door swings open easily.

Turn to PAGE 47.

Moving quickly, you grab the bottle of ink. You pull out the stopper and throw the contents in Dr. Lamprey's face.

For a moment, nothing happens. And then Dr. Lamprey begins to scream. He falls on the floor of the cave. His arms and legs are disappearing. As you watch, he turns into a long, wriggling creature, with a round mouth full of sharp, razorlike teeth. Screaming more faintly now, he wriggles away along the sand.

"That's one Lamprey that will never bother us again," laughs Uncle Dave. "A fitting end for such an evil man! And now, let's get to the beach."

Turn to *PAGE 86*.

You want to use the bottle of poison ink that the squid gave you. But you must stall for enough time to pull it out of your pocket.

"Wait!" you tell Dr. Lamprey. "I have an important message for you."

For a moment his eyes widen in interest. But only for a moment. You realize that the interest was not for your message, but for his belt. You watch as he presses one of the buttons on the belt.

And you watch as he releases it.

A strange, cold feeling has gone through your body. You start to ask Dr. Lamprey what he has done, but your mouth will not move.

Neither will any other part of your body. Sadly you realize that you have become one of Dr. Lamprey's artistic statues . . . and you wonder if you will be admired by the next person unlucky enough to visit Lost Island.

THE END

You pull the short switch. There is a brilliant flash of light and the room goes dark. Then, slowly, the lights begin to flicker back on. But there is something wrong with them.

You realize that you are seeing the lights from beneath the water. Then you realize that you are breathing. And only sea creatures can breathe underwater.

You give a tentative wiggle of your fins and swim around. In only a few strokes you bump your head against glass. You turn in the opposite direction, and again run into glass. With shock, you realize that you are inside a round bowl of water. In the reflection of the glass you can see that you have been turned into a bright orange goldfish! But you are not alone. A slightly larger goldfish is swimming beside you.

"I guess that was the wrong switch," says Uncle Dave.

"I guess so," you agree. Your voice sounds wavery underwater. But you know you'd better get used to it. You'd also better get used to being bored. For the first time in your life, you understand why goldfish spend all their time swimming around . . . and around . . . and around.

THE END

You press the green button. There is a sudden roaring noise, and you find yourself underwater. Quickly, you try to press the belt again.

But you can't figure out how to do it. Instead of hands, you now have suction cups! And the belt is no longer around your waist, because you don't have one.

In horror, you realize that you have turned yourself into an octopus!

You hope that Uncle Dave and Aunt Louise will manage to escape from Dr. Lamprey. But for now, all you can do is wave good-bye to them — with eight long tentacles.

THE END

The three of you step carefully into the rowboat. So far there is no sign of Dr. Lamprey. Dave begins to row, but it is tough going against the waves. You hear the sound of a motor and look behind you. Your blood freezes when you see Dr. Lamprey driving the cabin cruiser.

Dave rows even harder, but it is clear that it is only a matter of minutes before the evil scientist catches up to you.

Suddenly, in the distance, you see a group of small boats approaching. Your spirits lift when you recognize them as Coast Guard cruisers. If only you can reach them before Dr. Lamprey catches you.

Quick! Turn to PAGE 85.

The dolphin squeaks again. There is plenty of room for all of you to hold on to its back while it swims to shore. You realize that it is saving your lives — and then you remember why it seemed so familiar.

You heard dolphin squeaks like this once before — when Aunt Louise was in the glass cage. And now you realize that this must be the dolphin whose mind was in her body. This is the dolphin's way of thanking you for rescuing it from Dr. Lamprey.

For a moment you think of all the other sea creatures Dr. Lamprey enslaved. All of them, like the dolphin, have reason to be grateful to you. Suddenly the sea isn't such a cold and lonely place, after all.

THE END

"Okay, we'll do what you want," you say.

"Excellent," says Dr. Lamprey when he hears your decision. "Release them!" he orders the two sailors. "Now, stand over there," he tells you and Dave. He points to a spot along the wall.

"Good. These are the two survivors of a shipwreck, everyone got that? Okay, you two, look scared."

You and Dave exchange worried glances. Clearly this man is truly insane.

"No good," says Dr. Lamprey. "Look more scared. Ah, better. Now, LIGHTS!"

The room is suddenly lit with blindingly bright lights.

"CAMERA!" You hear a whirring and now realize that the strange projections on the bulkhead were cameras.

"ACTION!"

With that the room erupts into life. The pirate fights with the two sailors. The mermaid wiggles her tail. You realize that somehow you and Dave have gotten into the middle of a movie set. And you smile a moment before you go back to looking frightened. You are going to be a star!

THE END

The tide is with you, and you find your rowboat surrounded by the Coast Guard. A loud voice booms over a loudspeaker: "Stop right there! You're under arrest!"

You and Dave and Louise look at one another in puzzlement.

"Come on, Lamprey," says the voice. "Give up! And let the lady and the kid go."

"I'm not Dr. Lamprey," says Dave. He starts to explain who he is. At that moment there is the sound of a gunshot.

"He's over there!" shouts a young Coast Guard officer.

Two of the cutters take off after the cabin cruiser, which is now speeding back to the island.

Later, aboard the Coast Guard vessel, the captain apologizes. "We've been staking this island out for weeks," he says. "We figured anyone leaving it had to be Lamprey. He's a notorious smuggler. But we've got him. And we've got enough evidence to lock him up for a hundred years."

You and Dave exchange glances. No one says it, but you wonder if a hundred years will be long enough!

THE END

It is a beautiful, sunny day. The three of you walk along the beach, enjoying the fresh air. Uncle Dave and Aunt Louise are holding hands.

You look out into the bay and see the welcoming sight of a Coast Guard cutter. The three of you wave and shout, and soon you are aboard, safe and sound.

"We've been looking for you all day," says the captain. "We found the wreckage of the boat right away. Where have you been all this time?"

You and Dave exchange glances. You both know that he will never believe you.

"It's a long story, Captain," says Dave. "Let's just say that we spent some time exploring the island."

The captain looks at you and then shrugs. He orders his men to turn the boat for the mainland.

You and Dave and Louise watch as Lost Island rapidly becomes a speck in the distance.

THE END

"I'm not sure how I got here," says Louise. "I got in trouble swimming one day. I nearly drowned. When I woke up, I was in the hold of a boat. I heard the sailors talking. They were kidnapping me. I saw this island through the porthole. So I jumped overboard and swam here."

"Where are we?" says Uncle Dave.

"I don't know," says Louise. "There's nobody else on the island. But there's plenty to eat and a freshwater stream."

"I guess we'll wait for rescue together," says Uncle Dave. You can tell from his smile that he wouldn't mind waiting for years.

As for you . . . you're not so sure. You're happy for Uncle Dave and Aunt Louise. But you've never liked coconuts. Still, there could be advantages. You won't have to go to school while you're here. And while you're waiting for rescue, you'll be able to get the best suntan of your life.

THE END

"I'll ask the questions around here," says the bald man. "But for your information, I'm Dr. Lamprey, owner of Lost Island and captain of this submarine. You may address me as Sir."

"Tell your men to let us go!" says Dave. Then, sounding angry, he adds, "Sir."

"I will on one condition," says Dr. Lamprey. "Will you promise to cooperate, no matter what happens?"

"What if we don't?" you say.

"Then you'll walk the plank!" Dr. Lamprey begins laughing, his huge body shaking all over. The pirate and mermaid join in the laughter.

"I don't know what's going on, but these people are all crazy," Dave whispers.

You agree. You whisper back and forth, trying to decide if you can trust them. At last you reach a decision.

If you decide to promise to cooperate with Dr. Lamprey, turn to PAGE 84.

If you refuse go to PAGE 34.

"There are stranger things than pirates here," Hedwick replies. "In case you don't know it, you're on the private island of Dr. Lamprey. And now I think it's time for me to take him my catch of the day."

Hedwick takes the net down, with you and Dave still imprisoned in it. He throws you over his huge shoulders like a sack of potatoes and walks into the ocean.

"Watch it, Fatso!" says Dave. "I'm not about to let you drown us!"

"Have no fear of that," says Hedwick. "Though I'll wager you'll be sorry I didn't do it. Like I said, I'm taking you to Dr. Lamprey. And here he is now."

You hear the deep throbbing sound of a motor and a splashing noise. Then you see where Hedwick is taking you. Ahead, in the surf, you can see the top of a huge black submarine. Its hatch opens as you approach. With one quick motion, Hedwick turns the net upside down and dumps you and Uncle Dave into the submarine. You hear him laughing insanely as he swims away.

Turn to PAGE 62.

You have to stand on your tiptoes to see the symbol. It is a drawing of a long, eel-like creature with a large round mouth. The mouth is lined with sharp, pointed teeth.

You shiver in spite of yourself. "What is it?" you say.

"It's a drawing of a lamprey," replies your uncle, sounding grim. "Now I'm sure that this is Lost Island." After a moment he speaks again. "Come on," he says. "Let's see what's in the next room."

He walks through the large opening. You are about to follow him when you trip on a loose stone. Your flashlight goes flying through the narrow hole at the back of the cave.

"Come quick!" calls Dave. "You won't believe what's in here!"

Now you face a problem. Should you follow Dave? Or should you crawl through the small opening first to get your flashlight?

If you decide to follow Dave, turn to PAGE 36.

If you decide to get your flashlight first, go to PAGE 4.

You are in an underwater grotto. Half of the walls are lined with glass. Through the glass you can see exotic fish of all colors of the rainbow. Some are beautiful, some are monstrous. You realize that you are deep under water.

Turning, you notice that the room is full of dozens of glass cages. Imprisoned in these cages are human-sized creatures.

You see a pirate captain, his beard thick and long, a silver dagger between his teeth. In another cage is a mermaid, her beautiful red hair streaming down her back as she combs it with a brush made of golden shells. One glass cage is empty — and its door is wide open. With horror, you realize that the tortoise is carrying you toward it!

To find out what happens next, turn to PAGE 32.

You plunge into the pool and quickly feel the water closing over your face. As you swim, you try to remember the direction you came from. A swift current suddenly takes hold of you. When you can no longer hold your breath, you surface for air. There is no light, and you feel your hair brush hard rock as the water pushes you along.

The current moves in twists and turns, and you realize that you are lost in an underwater maze beneath the island.

Suddenly a faint light appears in the distance. The current sweeps you toward it. You surface and can see that there are two passages ahead in the maze. The light is coming from the one on the right.

Now you see a large, dark form looming in the lighted passage. Maybe the light means that there is dry land ahead. But you'll have to pass by the thing that is moving in the water to get there.

Which will it be? Will you take your chances and enter the lighted passage? If so, turn to PAGE 41.

If you decide to go on with the current, turn to PAGE 66.

"This is the only other way to defeat Lamprey," says the squid. It hands you a small bottle. "This is special ink," it says. "It is poisonous to Dr. Lamprey. If you splash it on him, he will be destroyed."

Thanking the squid, you turn to go. There are only two ways to get back to the grotto. One is to go back through the maze. The other takes you to the Cavern of the Eel.

Which will you choose? If you think you can outsmart the eel, turn to PAGE 67.

If you decide it's safer to take a chance on the maze, turn to PAGE 5.

Collect All the Twistaplot® Books

#1 *The Time Raider* by R. L. Stine
#2 *The Train of Terror* by Louise Munro Foley
#3 *The Formula for Trouble* by Megan Stine and H. William Stine
#4 *Golden Sword of Dragonwalk* by R. L. Stine
#5 *The Sinister Studios of KESP-TV* by Louise Munro Foley
#6 *Crash Landing* by Arthur Roth
#7 *The Video Avenger* by Douglas Colligan
#8 *Race Into the Past* by Megan Stine and H. William Stine
#9 *Horrors of the Haunted Museum* by R. L. Stine
#10 *Mission of the Secret Spy Squad* by Ruth Glick and Eileen Buckholtz
#11 *Camp-Out on Danger Mountain* by B. B. Hiller
#12 *Journey to Vernico 5* by Megan Stine and H. William Stine
#13 *Midnight at Monster Mansion* by Steven Otfinoski
#14 *Instant Millionaire* by R. L. Stine
#15 *Spellcaster* by Katy Brown
#16 *Secrets of the Lost Island* by Lynn Beach

Your collection won't be complete without:

#17 *Ghost Riders of Goldspur* by Barbara and Scott Siegel

You're visiting the Old West town of Goldspur when miraculously you are transported to Goldspur of the past! Now it's up to you to save the town from the vicious outlaw Harley brothers. Or maybe you'll decide to turn to the life of a Wild West desperado yourself!